Christmas Is Here!

By Siobhan Ciminera
Illustrated by SI Artists

Grosset & Dunlap

It's the berry best time of the year in Strawberryland— Christmastime!

Put Beginning Readers on the Right Track with
ALL ABOARD READING™

The All Aboard Reading series is especially designed for beginning readers. Written by noted authors and illustrated in full color, these are books that children really want to read—books to excite their imagination, expand their interests, make them laugh, and support their feelings. With fiction and nonfiction stories that are high interest and curriculum-related, All Aboard Reading books offer something for every young reader. And with four different reading levels, the All Aboard Reading series lets you choose which books are most appropriate for your children and their growing abilities.

Picture Readers
Picture Readers have super-simple texts, with many nouns appearing as rebus pictures. At the end of each book are 24 flash cards—on one side is a rebus picture; on the other side is the written-out word.

Station Stop 1
Station Stop 1 books are best for children who have just begun to read. Simple words and big type make these early reading experiences more comfortable. Picture clues help children to figure out the words on the page. Lots of repetition throughout the text helps children to predict the next word or phrase—an essential step in developing word recognition.

Station Stop 2
Station Stop 2 books are written specifically for children who are reading with help. Short sentences make it easier for early readers to understand what they are reading. Simple plots and simple dialogue help children with reading comprehension.

Station Stop 3
Station Stop 3 books are perfect for children who are reading alone. With longer text and harder words, these books appeal to children who have mastered basic reading skills. More complex stories captivate children who are ready for more challenging books.

In addition to All Aboard Reading books, look for All Aboard Math Readers™ (fiction stories that teach math concepts children are learning in school); All Aboard Science Readers™ (nonfiction books that explore the most fascinating science topics in age-appropriate language); All Aboard Poetry Readers™ (funny, rhyming poems for readers of all levels); and All Aboard Mystery Readers™ (puzzling tales where children piece together evidence with the characters).

All Aboard for happy reading!

Visit www.strawberryshortcake.com to join the Friendship Club and redeem your Strawberry Shortcake Berry Points for "berry" fun stuff!

GROSSET & DUNLAP
Published by the Penguin Group
Penguin Group (USA) Inc., 375 Hudson Street, New York, New York 10014, U.S.A.
Penguin Group (Canada), 10 Alcorn Avenue, Toronto, Ontario, Canada M4V 3B2
(a division of Pearson Penguin Canada Inc.)
Penguin Books Ltd, 80 Strand, London WC2R 0RL, England
Penguin Ireland, 25 St Stephen's Green, Dublin 2, Ireland
(a division of Penguin Books Ltd)
Penguin Group (Australia), 250 Camberwell Road, Camberwell, Victoria 3124, Australia
(a division of Pearson Australia Group Pty Ltd)
Penguin Books India Pvt Ltd, 11 Community Centre, Panchsheel Park,
New Delhi - 110 017, India
Penguin Group (NZ), Cnr Airborne and Rosedale Roads, Albany, Auckland 1310, New Zealand
(a division of Pearson New Zealand Ltd)
Penguin Books (South Africa) (Pty) Ltd, 24 Sturdee Avenue, Rosebank,
Johannesburg 2196, South Africa

Penguin Books Ltd, Registered Offices:
80 Strand, London WC2R 0RL, England

Library of Congress Cataloging-in-Publication Data

Ciminera, Siobhan.
Christmas is here! / by Siobhan Ciminera ; illustrated by SI Artists.
p. cm. — (All aboard reading. Station stop 1)
"Strawberry Shortcake."
Summary: Strawberry Shortcake loves sharing the holidays with her berry best friends,
but this year, when they are all busy, she leaves each one a gift and they are reminded
of the importance of spending Christmas together. Includes instructions
on making a sparkly strawberry ornament.
ISBN 0-448-43955-7 (pbk.)
[1. Christmas—Fiction. 2. Friendship—Fiction. 3. Gifts—Fiction.]
I. S.I. Artists (Group) II. Title. III. Series.
PZ7.C4917Chr 2005   [E]—dc22   2005003384

10 9 8 7 6 5 4 3 2 1

Strawberry Shortcake
hangs the stockings.

Strawberry Shortcake
puts out candy canes.

Strawberry Shortcake
hangs the wreath.

Strawberry Shortcake
needs to trim her tree.
It is a berry big job.

Strawberry Shortcake will
ask her friends to help!
It will be berry fun.

Angel Cake can't help.

She is busy making cards.

Huckleberry Pie can't help.

He is busy making fudge.

Ginger Snap can't help.
She is busy baking cookies.

Blueberry Muffin can't help.

She is busy wrapping presents.

Orange Blossom can't help.
She is busy baking a pie.

Strawberry's friends
can't come over.
So Strawberry will bring
Christmas fun to them!

Strawberry Shortcake goes to Cakewalk.

She gives Angel Cake
a pretty Christmas bell.

Strawberry Shortcake goes
to Huckleberry Briar.

She leaves a candy cane
for Huckleberry Pie.

Strawberry Shortcake
goes to Cookie Corners.

She gives Ginger Snap
a shiny snowflake.

Strawberry Shortcake goes
to Blueberry Valley.
She hangs a blue bow
on Blueberry Muffin's gate.

Strawberry Shortcake goes
to Orange Blossom Acres.

She leaves a sparkly star
for Orange Blossom.

Strawberry Shortcake goes back
to Strawberryland.

What's that?

Strawberry hears singing.

It is Strawberry's friends!
They are not too busy for
Christmas fun with her after all!

The kids help trim the tree.

Strawberry Shortcake
puts the star on top.

Berry merry Christmas,
Strawberry Shortcake!

Make your berry own sparkly strawberry Christmas ornament!

Make sure to get a grown-up's permission before making this berry fun craft!

<u>What you will need:</u>
2 pieces of white paper; red, green, and black crayons; scissors; glue stick; cotton balls; glitter; hole punch; red ribbon

1. Using your crayons, draw a strawberry on a piece of paper. (It's berry easy to make a strawberry. Just draw a heart and add leaves on top!) Put the blank piece of paper under the strawberry.

2. Ask an adult to help you cut out the strawberry—make sure you cut through both pieces of paper! You will have two strawberry shapes. Color the blank one in with your crayons.

3. Use the glue stick around the edges on the plain side of one strawberry. (Do not run the glue stick around the stem.) Attach it to the plain side of the other strawberry. Your strawberry should be open at the top.

4. Use the glue stick on the outside of your strawberry and pour glitter over it. Shake off the excess glitter.

5. Stuff your strawberry with cotton balls to make it puff out. Stop once you have filled it to the stem, and run the glue stick on the inside of the stem. Stick the two sides together.

6. Wait 5 minutes for the glue to dry.

7. Using your hole punch, make a hole in the stem.

8. Thread the ribbon through the hole and tie the ends together. Your ornament is ready to put on the tree!

Berry Merry Christmas!